DATE DUE

MAY 16	9/24		
MAY 20	12/1		
12/19	9/11		
10/20	10/17		
11/03			
10/29			
10/9			
11/6			
4/8			

DEMCO 128-5046

If You Give a Pig a Party

If You Give a Pig a Party

BY Laura Numeroff

ILLUSTRATED BY Felicia Bond

Laura Geringer Books
An Imprint of HarperCollins*Publishers*

If You Give a Pig a Party

Text copyright © 2005 by Laura Numeroff

Illustrations copyright © 2005 by Felicia Bond

Printed in the U.S.A. All rights reserved.

www.harperchildrens.com

Library of Congress Cataloging-in-Publication Data

Numeroff, Laura Joffe.

  If you give a pig a party / by Laura Numeroff ; illustrated by Felicia Bond.— 1st ed.

  p. cm.

  Summary: One thing leads to another when you give a pig a party.

  ISBN-10: 0-06-028326-2 — ISBN-10: 0-06-028327-0 (lib. bdg.)

  ISBN-13: 978-0-06-028326-1 — ISBN-13: 978-0-06-028327-8 (lib. bdg.)

  [1. Pigs—Fiction.] I. Bond, Felicia, ill. II. Title.

PZ7.N964Ic 2005

[E]—dc22   2003011799
                                                                            CIP
                                                                            AC

  4 5 6 7 8 9 10 ❖ First Edition

is a registered trademark of HarperCollins Publishers

If you give a pig a party,

she's going to ask for some balloons.

When you give her the balloons,
she'll want to decorate the house.

When she's finished,
she'll put on her favorite dress.

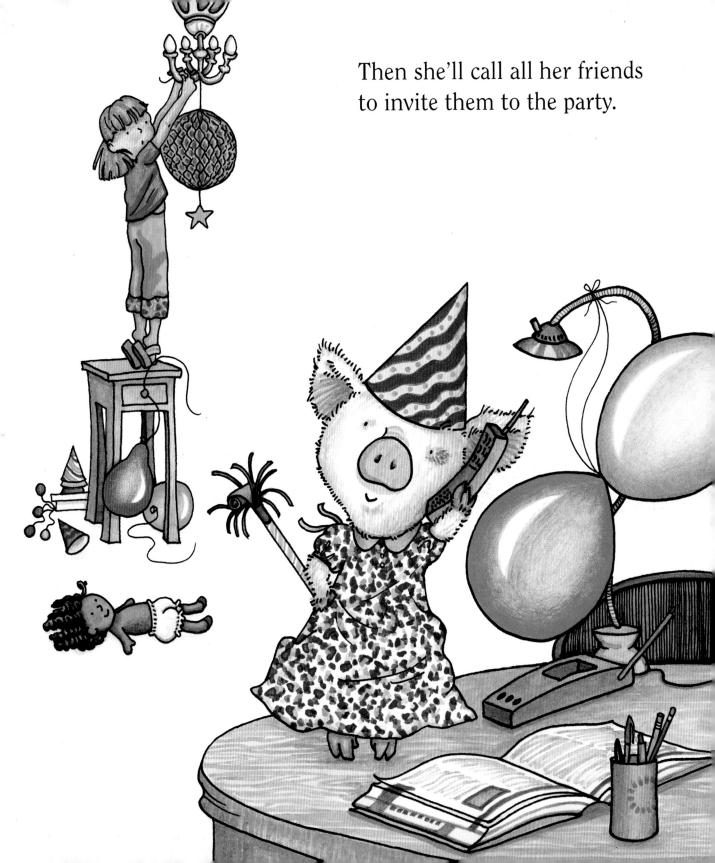

Then she'll call all her friends to invite them to the party.

Her friends won't be home,
so you'll go with her to look for them.

On the way, she'll see a street fair.

She'll want you to take her
on the bumper cars.

All her friends will be there.

Then you'll have to
take her on all the rides.

She'll want to play all the games, too.

When she's done, she'll ask you for some ice cream.

When she's finished eating the ice cream,
she'll need to change her clothes.
You'll have to take her home.

She'll ask her friends
to come along.

On the way, she'll start a game of hide-and-seek.

When you finally get home, you'll have to make dinner.

Then she'll want to have a sleepover.
You'll have to find pajamas

and blankets and pillows for everyone.

When she sees the pillows, she'll probably start a

pillow fight.

Then she'll make a
fortress out of blankets.

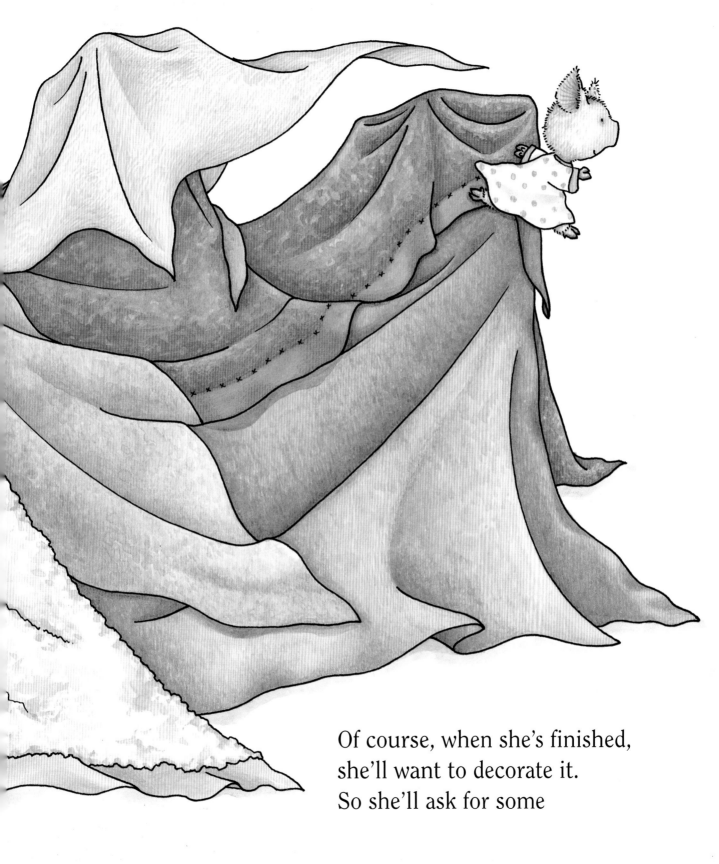

Of course, when she's finished,
she'll want to decorate it.
So she'll ask for some

balloons.

And chances are,

if you give her some balloons,

she's going to ask you
for a party.